For dear Esther, Alexandra and Elizabeth, Amazons all – S.P.C.

For sisters everywhere, and especially for my sister Charlotte,
who has all the qualities within – S.H.

First published in Great Britain in 2008 and in the USA in 2009 by
Frances Lincoln Children's Books, 4 Torriano Mews,
Torriano Avenue, London NW5 2RZ
www.franceslincoln.com

British Library Cataloguing in Publication Data available on request

ISBN: 978-1-84507-660-3

Illustrated with gouache and collage

Printed in China

1 3 5 7 9 8 6 4 2

Amazons!

Women Warriors of the World

Sally Pomme Clayton

Sophie Herxheimer

F

FRANCES LINCOLN
CHILDREN'S BOOKS

Contents

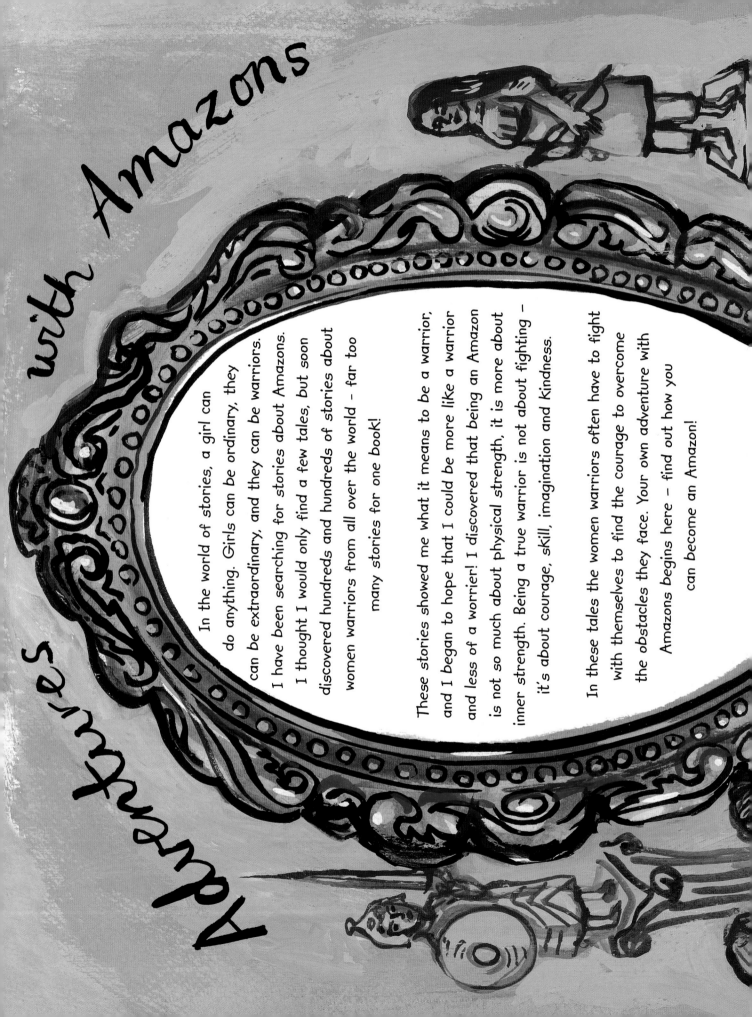

Adventures with Amazons

In the world of stories, a girl can do anything. Girls can be ordinary, they can be extraordinary, and they can be warriors. I have been searching for stories about Amazons. I thought I would only find a few tales, but soon discovered hundreds and hundreds of stories about women warriors from all over the world – far too many stories for one book!

These stories showed me what it means to be a warrior, and I began to hope that I could be more like a warrior and less of a worrier! I discovered that being an Amazon is not so much about physical strength, it is more about inner strength. Being a true warrior is not about fighting – it's about courage, skill, imagination and kindness.

In these tales the women warriors often have to fight with themselves to find the courage to overcome the obstacles they face. Your own adventure with Amazons begins here – find out how you can become an Amazon!

Queen of the Amazons

"Hercules," said King Eurystheus, "my daughter wants the golden belt that belongs to the Queen of the Amazons."

"But Amazons don't exist!" laughed Hercules.

"This is your ninth labour – my daughter wants the belt – and if you want to be a hero – get it!"

Hercules went down to the port. He chose a long, narrow boat that sat low in the water. A boat like this could weather storms, high seas and travel up-river. Then he spent the night pushing his way in and out of the crowded inns along the shore, offering a bag of gold to every sailor who would join his ship. By morning he had a crew of sixty, among them his friend the warrior Theseus.

Early the next morning, the crew took to their rowing benches, unfurled red sails and rowed out to sea. No one saw them leave except the King's daughter, watching from her window, her shining gold hair loose around her shoulders and her lips parted in a smile.

The sailors rowed for hours across the blue Aegean sea. The hours turned to days, as they stopped at islands to buy bread and wine, and to ask if anyone knew where the Amazons lived. People shook their heads. "Amazons are just a story!"

The ship arrived at the island of Crete, a place of ancient wisdom where the great god Zeus had been born. Hercules and Theseus sat in the shade of a tree and an old woman served them honey cakes.

"I know what you're looking for," she whispered. "Go north, through the Golden Horn, and north again into the Black Sea. You will find the Amazon fortress there."

Hercules was beginning to feel nervous.

"Can women really be warriors?" he wondered.

They sailed northwards and entered the Black Sea. The water was calm and they travelled close to the coast. They saw farms and villages dotted along the shore. They saw shepherds tending their sheep and mountains thick with walnut trees. But they did not see an Amazon fortress.

Dusk fell, and the lookout boy called from his post, "Captain Hercules! A light, sir, in the distance." He pointed to something gleaming in the evening sun.

The sailors pulled hard at their oars, rowing towards the light. As they drew closer, the light became a castle, a castle made entirely of copper. The castle had vast copper walls, soaring towers and massive gates made of beaten copper decorated with spiral patterns. But the towers had no doors and the gates were shut fast.

"Only giants could have built such a fortress," said Hercules.

They pulled the ship around the bay and dropped anchor so that they could spy on the castle in secret. The sailors passed round flagons of wine and watched the castle glinting under the stars. One by one, their eyes closed and they fell asleep, so deeply asleep that they did not hear the sound of oars stroking water.

Melanippe rowed softly, dipping her oars carefully into the sea. She drew her boat alongside the ship, then, silent as a cat, climbed up a rope, over the side of the ship and lightly on to the deck. There was a sound of snoring and grunting and the strong smell of wine. Melanippe slipped through the shadows and passed the sleeping sailors, wondering who they were.

One blonde-haired sailor was lying face down. As Melanippe quietly stepped over his body, he suddenly reached out and grabbed her ankle.

"What have we here?" said Theseus, rolling on to his side to inspect his catch. Seeing a girl with a dagger at her waist, he quickly bound her wrists and marched her to Hercules.

"Look what I've found!" he boasted.

Hercules lit a lantern.

"What is your name?" he asked.

"Melanippe – it means 'black horse'."

"What are you doing here?" said Hercules.

"I'm an Amazon. This is my country." Her dark eyes flashed. "What are *you* doing here?"

"I have come for the Queen of the Amazons' belt."

Melanippe laughed,

"Queen Hippolyta's belt? Impossible! Hippolyta is the daughter of a god. Her father is Ares, god of war and he gave her the belt. All knowledge and power is in that belt. Hippolyta will never part with it."

"Tie her up!" shouted Hercules. "Let's see if the Queen would rather part with her belt – or one of her Amazons."

Theseus tied Melanippe to the mast of the ship.

"You can't treat me like this!" she cried. "You can't tie me up just because I live by the Amazon code."

"Amazons have a code?" said Theseus, turning to the sailors, laughing. "What could that be?"

"To be honest and true," said Melanippe.

The sailors fell silent.

"We are taught to be warriors from an early age. We learn the skills of archery, riding, combat and debate. We never fight unless we have to, but we are always ready – ready to protect our castle and our code. We marry and have families, just like you, but only when we have done our duty as warriors."

Hercules felt uneasy and placed his hand on his sword. So Amazons were not just a story.

Behind the copper gates, smoke curled into the dawn sky. Hippolyta, Queen of the Amazons threw leaves and berries on to a fire. She moved round the fire chanting, and the belt of gold wrapped round her waist like a snake flashed in the firelight. "Artemis, goddess of freedom," she prayed, "return Melanippe to us. Bring her back without a battle."

The Amazons stood in a circle and the reedy sound of a bagpipe filled the air. The Amazons lifted moon-shaped shields above their heads and began to dance the Shield Dance – taking slow rhythmic steps, stamping, turning, shouting, moving perfectly in unison. They rubbed poison on to the tips of their arrows, passing a shell from hand to hand, dipping their arrowheads into an oily mixture of death. They were ready for anything and afraid of nothing.

The massive copper gates swung open and the Amazons poured out, dragging ships and pulling chariots, some with dogs at their side, some with spears, all with quivers rattling on their backs. They set sail, the Queen of the Amazons standing tall in the prow of the largest ship.

The lookout boy rubbed his eyes in disbelief. Moving steadily across the sea was a long line of boats!

"Attack, attack!" he shouted to the sleeping crew.

The sailors leapt into action, loosing arrows and hurling spears at the Amazon boats. In the lead boat Phoebe, Asteria and Tecmessa were struck and fell into the sea. The Amazon army fought hard, their arrows swift, their shots deadly.

They pulled their boats alongside Hercules' ship

and jumped aboard. They ran through the boat, found Melanippe and set her free. They fought a terrible battle, but the sailors were no match for the strength and lightness of the women. Leaving Theseus injured and half the crew dead, the Amazons jumped back into their boats and turned for home.

Then Hercules saw something gold flashing from one of the ships. He climbed the lookout post and saw a proud woman with a shining gold belt around her waist.

"That belt is mine!" he cried. He drew his fastest arrow and took aim. The arrow whistled through the air and struck Queen Hippolyta in the heart.

Hercules pulled his ship close to Hippolyta's and leapt aboard. Hippolyta was lying wounded on the deck.

"Take the belt, Hercules," she gasped, "if it is so important to you."

Hercules knelt and unclasped the golden belt. As he removed it, he looked into Hippolyta's face. She had green eyes that seemed to contain the whole earth and red hair that framed her face like a halo.

Hercules felt a sharp pain in his heart: the Queen of the Amazons had the most beautiful face he had ever seen. He grabbed the belt and returned to his own ship.

Hippolyta's breathing grew weaker and weaker. She had lost so much blood that before the Amazons could carry their queen back to her castle, she was dead.

Hercules set sail for home. It was a sombre journey; he had lost half his men in the battle. But he had the belt. He ran the fine gold belt through his fingers during the day, and slept with it under his pillow at night. Some say he was never happy again, and spent the rest of his life longing for the Queen of the Amazons.

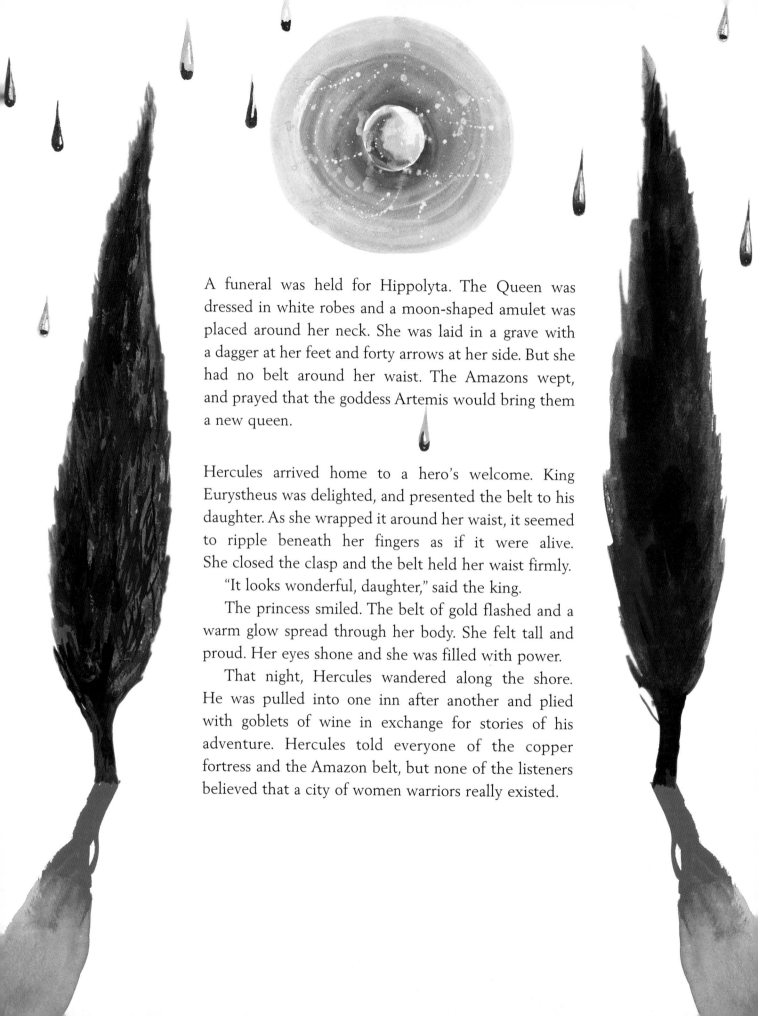

A funeral was held for Hippolyta. The Queen was dressed in white robes and a moon-shaped amulet was placed around her neck. She was laid in a grave with a dagger at her feet and forty arrows at her side. But she had no belt around her waist. The Amazons wept, and prayed that the goddess Artemis would bring them a new queen.

Hercules arrived home to a hero's welcome. King Eurystheus was delighted, and presented the belt to his daughter. As she wrapped it around her waist, it seemed to ripple beneath her fingers as if it were alive. She closed the clasp and the belt held her waist firmly.

"It looks wonderful, daughter," said the king.

The princess smiled. The belt of gold flashed and a warm glow spread through her body. She felt tall and proud. Her eyes shone and she was filled with power.

That night, Hercules wandered along the shore. He was pulled into one inn after another and plied with goblets of wine in exchange for stories of his adventure. Hercules told everyone of the copper fortress and the Amazon belt, but none of the listeners believed that a city of women warriors really existed.

The next day, confusion broke out. The king's daughter was missing. King Eurystheus looked everywhere. He ordered the whole kingdom to be searched. Hercules and his warriors hunted night and day, but they did not find the princess. She had vanished, and no one knew where she had gone.

Then a rumour went round: an old sailor had seen the princess climbing aboard a ship. No one knew if this was a fact, or just a tale. But the King never saw his daughter again.

Not long after that, a boat arrived from the Black Sea with more rumours: the Amazon belt had been returned, and the Amazons had a new, golden-haired queen.

Amazons – fact or tale ?

Warrior women appear throughout ancient Greek mythology. One of the first tales about Amazons was written down in about 750 BC by Homer in *The Iliad*, where he describes how Amazons fought at the battle of Troy. But there are stories about warrior women all over the world. The Celts had a battle goddess, Morrigane, who flew over the battlefield in the form of a crow. The Japanese sun goddess, Ama Terasu, wore armour and was a skilful swordswoman. Sakhmet was an Egyptian goddess, a ferocious fighter with the head of a lion.

Warrior women appear in tales again and again, as popular as witches and princesses. But were these Amazons just tales – or did they really exist?

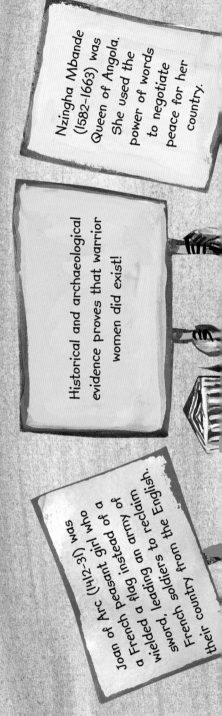

Nzingha Mbande (1582-1663) was Queen of Angola. She used the power of words to negotiate peace for her country.

Historical and archaeological evidence proves that warrior women did exist!

Joan of Arc (1412-31) was a French peasant girl who wielded a flag instead of a sword, leading an army of a French girl who reclaim their country from the English.

Graves belonging to female warriors and leaders, dating from 750–300 BC, have been found in the Ukraine, the Caucusus, China and Mongolia.

Stories of women warriors have one foot in history, and one foot in mystery, a place where fact and tale intertwine.

Αμαζόνες

Zenobia ruled Syria in the 3rd century AD. She commanded a powerful army, only addressing them when she was wearing armour!

Queen Boudicca mounted her chariot and went to war to defend the British against the Romans in AD 61.

'A fact is a fact,
a tale is a tale,
but where no one passed by
there runs no trail.
What was not planted
bears no seed,
what did not happen
no rumour breed.' RUSSIAN SAYING

Dragon Girl

"That's it for another year," muttered Farmer Li.

His seven daughters went back to their weaving and sewing. But his wife was upset,

"Don't you think we should leave?" she said. "All the other families with daughters have left."

Farmer Li shook his head,

"We have farmed this land for generations. Our life is here. We can't leave."

"And what if it's our turn next?" asked his wife.

"Well, we have a whole year before the dragon must be fed again," said Li. "Let's hope he disappears."

Every year the dragon had to be fed. And every year the Emperor chose the girl who would be taken to the top of the mountain and left outside the dragon's cave. Every year a weeping family would hope the dragon had disappeared. And every year their hopes would be dashed, when they found their daughter had become the dragon's girl and she had been devoured.

A band of warriors went to kill the dragon, but returned terrified, saying the monster was impossible to kill – it had seven heads and seven tails and a body that stretched the length of a whole mountain! No one was brave enough to fight the dragon after that. And no one went near the mountain unless they were ordered to take their daughter there.

Farmer Li dug the sticky ground and planted a new crop of rice. He kept the fields flooded with just the right amount of water, and tended his rice seedlings with care. The months passed, and he watched with pride as green stalks of rice shot up from their watery bed. When the rice was ripe, Li's wife and daughters joined the working party, cutting the grain, threshing it and filling the sacks for market.

A year passed, and the dragon had not disappeared. The Emperor looked about for a girl to feed the dragon, but all the families with daughters had left town. There was only one family with girls left.

Farmer Li was called to the Imperial Palace.

"You have seven daughters," declared the Emperor. "You can afford to lose one. But since you feed us all with such delicious rice, I will allow you to choose which of your daughters shall be the dragon's girl."

Farmer Li returned home with a heavy heart. He sat in silence at the dinner table and did not touch his bowl of steaming noodles.

His daughters made jokes, but Li did not smile.

"What's the matter?" asked his wife. "Are you ill?"

Li pushed the bowl to one side.

"It is our turn," he said. "One of our daughters is to be the dragon's girl. And the worst of it is – I must choose."

His youngest daughter, Chi, stood up.

"Father," she said, "you can't choose. That is too cruel. I will go. I am the youngest. My older sisters are ready to marry, but I have nothing to lose. Send me."

天
保

That night Chi went to the shrine at the back of the house. She placed a tiny bowl of rice on the altar for the goddess Tianhou, Empress of Heaven. The shrine glittered with candles, lighting up the goddess's red dress and crown of shooting stars.

Chi bent her head and whispered, "Empress of Heaven who protects those in trouble, I need your help. Give me your courage. Make me brave. Goddess Tianhou, whose spirit helps all, help me now."

As Chi knelt silently before the shrine, an idea floated into her mind. It was a strange, scary idea. But Chi knew Tianhou had given her the idea, so she bowed and thanked the goddess. Chi hoped she could trust the idea, and trust herself to carry it out.

Early the next morning Chi smiled at her weeping family,

"Don't worry," she said, "I'll be back." And she set off for the Emperor's palace alone.

"I will be the dragon's girl," she said to the Emperor, "if you give me seven barrels of sticky rice, seven barrels of strong wine and a sharp sword."

The Emperor laughed.

"You won't be the one doing the eating, little miss, but very well."

Chi climbed into a cart loaded with barrels of rice and wine. And a lonely donkey pulled the cart over hills and up into the rugged mountains. All the time Chi held the Emperor's sword tight in her hand, hoping it would make her brave enough to carry out Tianhou's idea. Then Chi saw a dark hole in the side of a mountain, billowing out black smoke – the dragon's cave.

Chi unhitched the donkey and set it free. She placed the barrels of sticky rice and strong wine in a long, winding line, and hid behind a rock.

There was a rumble and the ground began to shake. Out of the cave lumbered seven green scaly heads, seven jaws with razor teeth and fourteen blood-red eyes. Chi was so terrified, she could hardly breathe, but she thought of Tianhou and felt calmer. The dragon was so fat, he could no longer fly, and so ancient, his back was covered with moss and fir trees.

He dragged his body out of the cave, uncoiling seven sharp, pointed tails, stretching himself out to the length of a whole mountain.

"Perhaps this monster *is* impossible to kill," shuddered Chi, but she thought of Tianhou and felt stronger.

The dragon lifted his seven heads and sniffed the air. He licked seven crusty mouths with seven green slimy tongues, and slithered towards the barrels. The dragon sniffed the first barrel, put his first head inside and gobbled up all the rice. The dragon moved on to the second barrel, shoved his second head inside and gorged himself on rice. He moved on to the next barrel, and the next, greedily gobbling up all seven barrels of sticky rice.

Chi watched, hoping the dragon would be thirsty.

The dragon lumbered over to the barrels of wine. He pushed his first head inside the first barrel and gulped down the wine, then lifted his head and looked about, dazed. His two red eyes rolled, blinked and shut tight. He staggered to the second barrel, thrust in his second head and guzzled down the wine. Two more red eyes closed.

The dragon drank seven barrels of strong wine and his fourteen red eyes blinked and closed fast. Then he sank to the ground in a deep, drunken sleep.

"Tianhou," whispered Chi. "Help me now."

Chi leapt out from behind the rock, and raised the sword.

Using all her strength, she brought the sword down and sliced off the dragon's first head. The dragon gave a thundering roar, twelve eyes rolled in their sockets, six mouths snapped, and Chi leapt backwards.

"I must be quick," she thought. "And I must trust myself." Chi lifted the sword and swung it again, and again, and again…
She sliced off

two, three, four, five, six, all seven of the dragon's heads!

The dragon was dead! But just to be sure, Chi raised the sword and sliced off the dragon's seven tails. As she sliced off the seventh tail, she saw something glittering inside. She cut the tail open, and buried inside were rubies, diamonds and lumps of gleaming jade. The dragon's tail was full of jewels!

Chi piled the jewels into the cart and set off down the mountain, pulling the cart behind her. When she came to the foothills, she saw a group of people weeping and wailing. It was her father, mother and six sisters.

"I told you not to worry," cried Chi.

Farmer Li wiped his eyes. His lovely, smiling daughter was alive!

"It's a miracle," he said. "My seventh daughter has killed the seven-headed dragon!"

Farmer Li hugged Chi.

"You did not become the dragon's girl," he said, "because you are the Dragon Girl."

Farmer Li and his family stayed in the land they loved, and the dragon's jewels kept them rich for the rest of their lives.

The whole country celebrated the courage of the girl who killed the dragon. And Chi is still remembered today in a song which tells the story of Chi, daughter of Li, the Dragon Girl.

Travel through the dragon and find the treasure.

Amazon Game

START

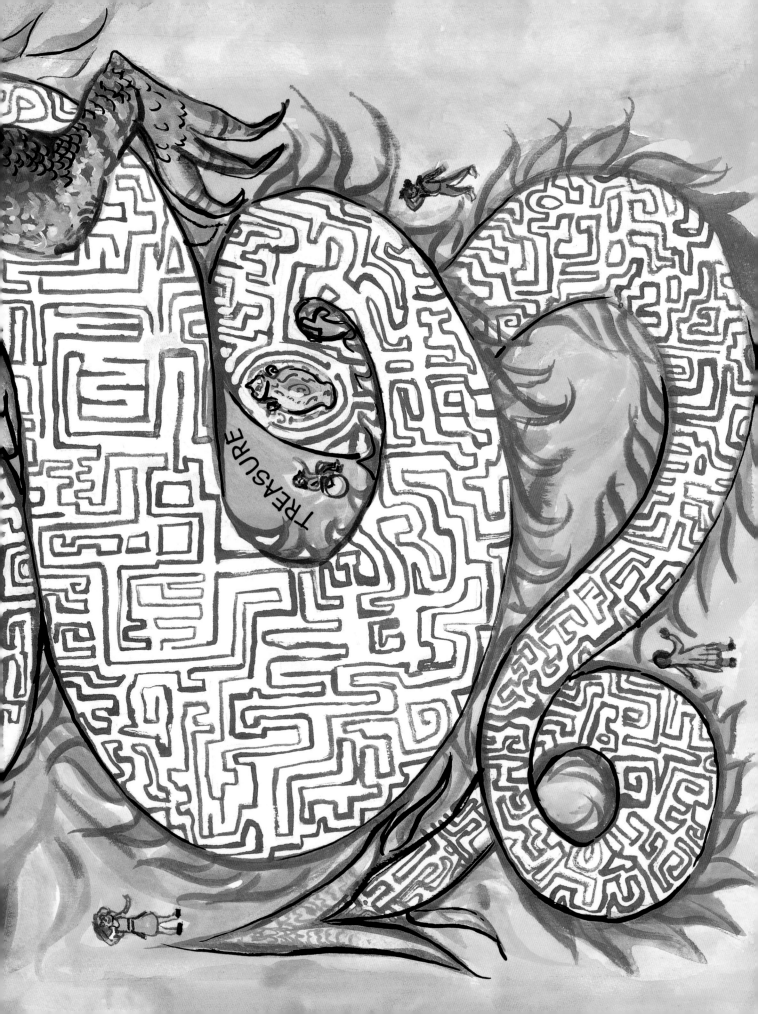

TREASURE

Winning Eagle Feathers

The Chief of the Sioux had a beautiful daughter. Her name was Magaskawee – which means 'graceful' – and it suited her. She was as tall and straight as a pine tree, with long black plaits and rosy red cheeks. And by the time she was seventeen, all the young men of the tribe wanted to marry her.

Chayton was always giving Magaskawee presents. He would go on raiding campaigns against the Crow tribe and bring back necklaces, weapons and fine horses. Magaskawee listened to Chayton's warrior tales, but she never accepted his gifts.

Little Eagle watched from afar. He loved Magaskawee too, but kept silent. He did not have gifts to give. He only had a tiny pony, and he was not brave at all.

When Chayton asked for Magaskawee's hand in marriage, she did not reply. At the next tribal meeting she stepped into the circle and announced:

"Father Chief, People of the Sioux, I cannot get married until I have counted coup for my brothers, my three brothers who died fighting. I must count coup for them before I do anything else."

The Chief looked stern, but said nothing. And a low murmur went around the tribe.

The battlefield was a place of honour. Killing an enemy was considered cowardly – tribes believed it was more important for a warrior to show courage and skill. So instead of killing their enemies, warriors counted coup. They would sneak up on an enemy, gently touch them, then escape without being caught. For each coup counted, a warrior would win an eagle feather to wear in his hair. Warriors who had counted many coups had headdresses thick with eagle feathers. And only when a warrior had counted coup, could he boast of his adventures round the campfire.

That night, the Chief spoke to his daughter.

"Magaskawee, a girl cannot count coup. Girls don't win eagle feathers."

"Well, they do now," said Magaskawee. "I must count coup for my brothers."

The Chief shook his head,

"I have already lost your three brothers in battle, and your dear mother

in childbirth. You are all I have left, and I might lose you too. I beg you, don't go."

"I would rather go with your blessing, Father, but if I have to, I will go without."

The Chief walked to the back of the tepee and opened a wooden chest. He lifted out a bright stick decorated with beads and feathers.

"Then take my coup stick. It has seen many coups. I ask just one thing – bring it back!"

The next morning, Magaskawee prepared to ride to the enemy camp. She painted her horse's coat with yellow hailstone spots and white lightning flashes to give it power. She put on her mother's soft buckskin dress and plaited her hair, tying a small green stone into the braid to protect her from harm.

Magaskawee rode along the sagebrush path, across the flat green prairie and through the waving grass of the Great Plains. She rode all day, until she passed the canyon of burnt rocks and entered Crow territory.

Magaskawee tied up her horse, got down on her hands and knees, and crawled into the Crow camp. A young boy was rubbing down his horse. Magaskawee reached out with her coup stick and gently touched him on the shoulder.

The boy jumped.

"Who's there!" he cried, looking around. But he could not see anyone. He hoped he had not been touched by a coup stick – it was such a disgrace to have coup counted against you.

Magaskawee tiptoed through a glade of trees. A warrior was lying beside his tepee, fast asleep. Magaskawee lightly brushed her coup stick over his forehead.

The man rubbed his face, as if an insect had crawled over his nose, but there was nothing there. He opened his eyes and looked about suspiciously – he hadn't been touched by a coup stick, had he?

Magaskawee climbed a tree and silently slid along a branch. The Crow Chief was sitting by the fire smoking his pipe. She lowered her arm and tapped the Chief on his head.

"What was that!" cried the Crow Chief, leaping to his feet and looking about – someone had counted coup!

"Gather a war party!" he called. "We are under attack."

Magaskawee was already riding away, holding her coup stick high and urging her horse on, when an arrow struck her horse's flank. Her horse stumbled and sank to the ground. Magaskawee heard whoops and war cries and quickly hid under a clump of bushes. She lay still, trying to quieten her breathing, as a band of Crow warriors passed by,

"The horse is dead," they shouted. "We must kill the rider. No one counts coup against the Crow." And they galloped on.

Magaskawee waited until there was silence, then set off on foot, slipping unnoticed between the trees.

Back at Sioux camp, the Chief waited for his daughter to return. As night fell, he heard war cries. Chayton and the best Sioux warriors leapt on to their swiftest horses and raced towards the Crow tribe.

Little Eagle watched them ride away. He only had a tiny pony, and he was not brave at all. But he thought of Magaskawee, all alone and maybe in trouble. Without wondering if he was brave enough, Little Eagle mounted his pony and rode towards the arrows and the smoke, looking for Magaskawee.

Little Eagle left the battle, and his tribe, far behind. He rode under the moon and under the stars, looking for Magaskawee. Suddenly he heard a soft whistle echoing through the darkness. It sounded just like Magaskawee's secret sound! Little Eagle put his hands to his mouth and made his own secret sound in reply, hooting like an owl. The whistle answered back, and Magaskawee stepped out of the bushes.

"Little Eagle!" she said, throwing her arms around his neck, "I am so glad to see you!"

Little Eagle felt happier than he had ever felt before. But there was no time to waste. "Take my horse," he said urgently. "Ride home as fast as you can!"

Magaskawee mounted the horse and made room for Little Eagle to climb up beside her. Little Eagle shook his head. "My pony is not strong enough to carry us both. I will follow on foot."

"I can't leave you!" cried Magaskawee.

But Little Eagle reached out, struck the pony, and it reared up and galloped towards home.

When Magaskawee arrived, her father hugged her tightly.

"You brought my coup stick back!" he said. "And you have won your eagle feathers."

The tribe gathered round to hear Magaskawee's adventures. But Magaskawee would not speak until Little Eagle had returned.

Dawn broke, and there was no sign of Little Eagle. So Chayton rode out again. Halfway along the sagebrush path he came upon a body lying face down in the grass with an arrow lodged in its back. Chayton rolled the body to one side. It was Little Eagle. The arrow had killed him.

Chayton knelt beside Little Eagle and whispered a prayer to the Great Spirit. Then he picked up Little Eagle's body, placed it on his horse's back and rode home.

The Sioux tribe honoured the life and mourned the death of Little Eagle with a sacred ceremony. Then, at last, Magaskawee spoke:

"Father Chief, People of the Sioux, a warrior does not always feel brave, but a true warrior does not let fear stop them. Little Eagle was afraid, yet he set out to find me. Little Eagle thought he had nothing to give, yet he gave me his pony, walked home in my place and gave the greatest gift of all – his life. Little Eagle did not think he was brave at all, yet he became a true warrior."

At the next tribal meeting, Magaskawee was honoured as the first girl who had counted coup. She was presented with three eagle feathers – one for each of her brothers. She wore the feathers proudly in her hair. But when it came to boasting of her adventures around the campfire, Magaskawee would not tell the story of how she had won her eagle feathers. Instead, she spoke of the eagle she had lost, Little Eagle, and how he was the bravest warrior of all.

Did Magaskawee count coup for Little Eagle, and win a feather for him?

Well, that's another story…

Spot the Amazon!

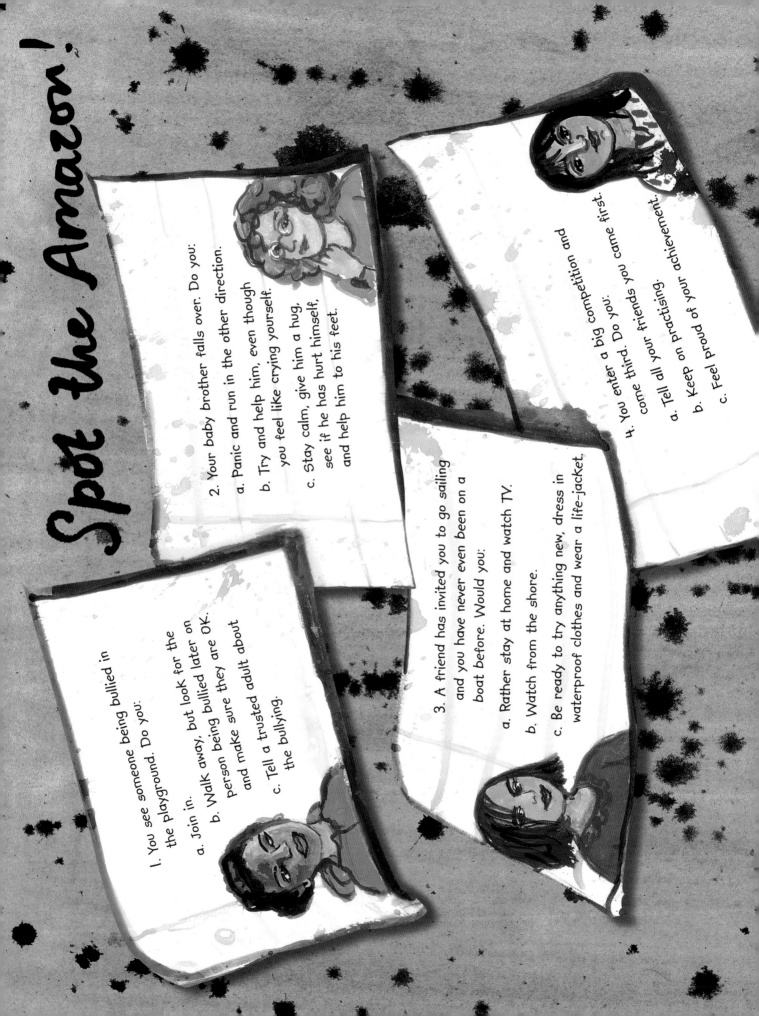

1. You see someone being bullied in the playground. Do you:

 a. Join in.

 b. Walk away, but look for the person being bullied later on and make sure they are OK.

 c. Tell a trusted adult about the bullying.

2. Your baby brother falls over. Do you:

 a. Panic and run in the other direction.

 b. Try and help him, even though you feel like crying yourself.

 c. Stay calm, give him a hug, see if he has hurt himself, and help him to his feet.

3. A friend has invited you to go sailing and you have never even been on a boat before. Would you:

 a. Rather stay at home and watch TV.

 b. Watch from the shore.

 c. Be ready to try anything new, dress in waterproof clothes and wear a life-jacket.

4. You enter a big competition and come third. Do you:

 a. Tell all your friends you came first.

 b. Keep on practising.

 c. Feel proud of your achievement.

5. You have dinner at your friend's house, but your plate is full of food you've never eaten before. Would you:

    a. Turn your nose up and refuse to eat it.

    b. Push the food around your plate so it looks as if you're eating.

    c. Taste a small mouthful of food and discover the meal is delicious.

6. Your beloved pet has died. Do you:

    a. Try not to cry, in case people think you are weak.

    b. Cry in secret.

    c. Openly show how much you loved and miss your pet.

7. Your Grandmother climbs stairs very slowly. Do you:

    a. Push ahead of her and tell her she's a slow-coach.

    b. Walk slowly and patiently behind her.

    c. Walk beside her, offering to help her if she needs it.

Durga

Once there was a demon who was so bad, he wanted to take over the Universe. He turned himself into a massive buffalo – a monster with red eyes and shaggy black hair: the Buffalo Demon. For a thousand years he chanted the spell of immortality, until it was impossible for any man to kill him.

Then the Buffalo Demon took over. He raged across the Earth, crumbling mountains beneath his hooves and whipping oceans into tidal waves with his tail, blowing away cities with a snort and scooping up people with his horns. Every living thing was terrified. Rivers changed their course. Fire lost its strength. Even the stars fled away.

When the Buffalo Demon had destroyed Earth, he set about taking over Heaven. He charged into Heaven, roaring and bellowing, forcing the gods to bow down and worship him.

Demon-Slayer

The gods stood firm and refused, so the Buffalo Demon picked them up by his horns and tossed them out of Heaven.

The gods tumbled down to Earth, into a forest where they were forced to live like mere human beings.

"This is wrong," they cried, "gods living on Earth and demons living in Heaven! The universe has been turned upside down by this terrible demon, and even the gods can't stop him."

The gods were filled with anger. They screwed up their faces in fury. They frowned, squeezing their eyes, knitting their brows and gritting their teeth in rage.

"Someone must slay this demon!"

The gods shone with rage. Their anger united in a flash. Blazing energy burst from their faces and a brilliant flame lit up the sky. The flame flickered – something was being born.

Out of the flame stepped a woman. A radiant woman. She had three eyes, ten arms, and skin the colour of gold. The gods' anger had created a goddess – the beautiful, fiery Durga.

Durga Demon-Slayer, born to kill!

Durga smiled at the gods and spoke in a sweet voice.

"The Buffalo Demon cannot be killed by a man, but there is nothing to stop a woman!"

The gods armed Durga. Each gave her a different weapon:

Indra, God of Sky – a thunderbolt,

Vayu, Lord of Wind – a bow,

Suraya, the Sun – arrows,

Vishnu, Protector – his own silver discus,

Varuna, God of Water – a conch shell,

Shiva, Destroyer – his pointed trident,

Agni, Fire God – flaming spears,

Yama, God of Death – his noose,

Kala, Lord of Time – a sword,

and Brahma, the Creator – a magic drinking-cup, always brimful of wine.

Then the gods dressed Durga in shining garments which would never wear out, placed gold around her neck, and gave her a hundred rings, one for each finger. And the snowy Himalayan Mountains sent a golden tiger for Durga to ride into battle.

The new goddess threw back her head and laughed. Her three eyes could see past, present and future. She was wisdom and warrior combined. Her laugh echoed across the universe. Durga, the Flaming One, was more dangerous than all the gods and demons put together! She climbed on to the back of the tiger, and rode off to meet the Buffalo Demon.

"What is that noise?" roared the Buffalo Demon. "Who dares upset my kingdom?"

The Buffalo Demon's army of little devils rushed backwards and forwards trying to discover who was making the terrible noise.

STABBING

HITTING

SPIKING

SLICING

BLASTING

BURNING

HANGING

48

SLASHING

SHOOTING

DROWNING

Then they saw a light shining in the distance, a light so bright, they had to shield their little red eyes. As the light came closer, the Buffalo Demon snorted, "Have no fear, demons – it's just a woman. A beautiful woman, but only a woman. Kill her!"

The devils swarmed over Durga, biting and scratching. Durga stood still, her face serene, and suddenly her ten arms rotated and her ten weapons flashed like cosmic fireworks.

Durga calmly cut through the demons, smiling peacefully, while all around her was total destruction. Durga sighed, and her sigh turned into an army of warrior maidens who marched across the world slaying every demon in sight. Durga had become a killing machine and no one could stop her. The demon army was destroyed and the Buffalo Demon was left alone.

"You are a woman!" bellowed the Buffalo Demon. "A powerful woman, but only a woman!"

He pounded the earth with his hooves and lowered his horns. Durga flicked her noose. The rope whirled through the air, caught the Buffalo Demon by his horns, wrapped around his body and bound him tight.

Instantly the Buffalo Demon turned into a lion with razor teeth and claws. The lion tore the noose and, snarling and roaring, leapt at Durga. The Goddess drew her sword and sliced off the lion's head.

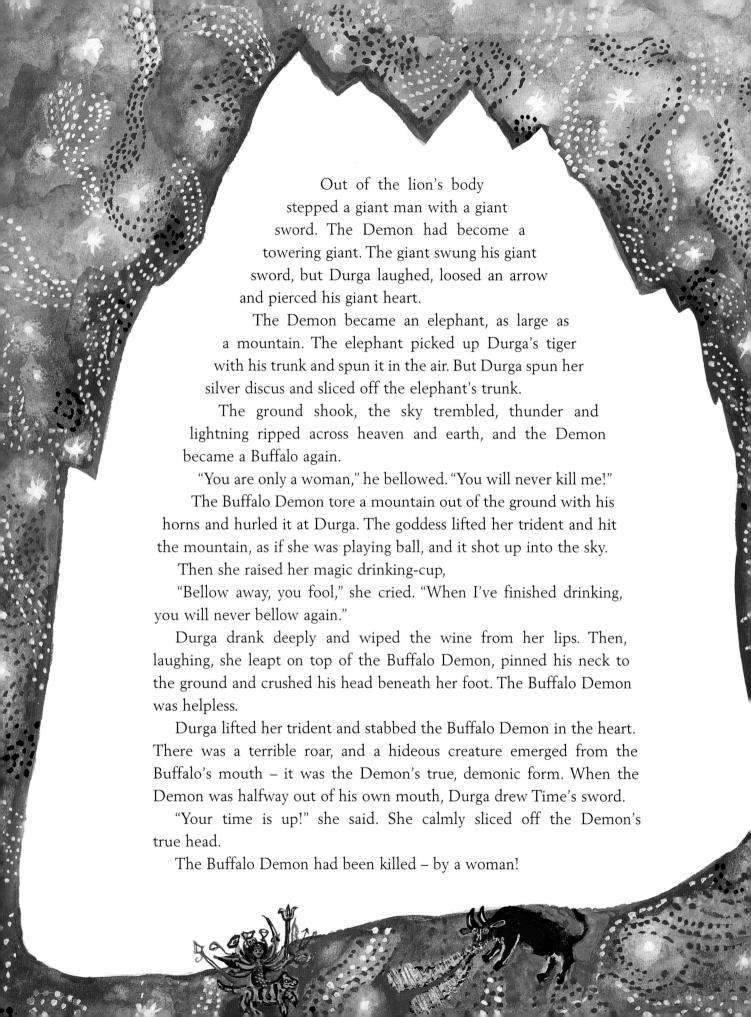

Out of the lion's body
stepped a giant man with a giant
sword. The Demon had become a
towering giant. The giant swung his giant
sword, but Durga laughed, loosed an arrow
and pierced his giant heart.

The Demon became an elephant, as large as
a mountain. The elephant picked up Durga's tiger
with his trunk and spun it in the air. But Durga spun her
silver discus and sliced off the elephant's trunk.

The ground shook, the sky trembled, thunder and
lightning ripped across heaven and earth, and the Demon
became a Buffalo again.

"You are only a woman," he bellowed. "You will never kill me!"

The Buffalo Demon tore a mountain out of the ground with his
horns and hurled it at Durga. The goddess lifted her trident and hit
the mountain, as if she was playing ball, and it shot up into the sky.

Then she raised her magic drinking-cup,

"Bellow away, you fool," she cried. "When I've finished drinking,
you will never bellow again."

Durga drank deeply and wiped the wine from her lips. Then,
laughing, she leapt on top of the Buffalo Demon, pinned his neck to
the ground and crushed his head beneath her foot. The Buffalo Demon
was helpless.

Durga lifted her trident and stabbed the Buffalo Demon in the heart.
There was a terrible roar, and a hideous creature emerged from the
Buffalo's mouth – it was the Demon's true, demonic form. When the
Demon was halfway out of his own mouth, Durga drew Time's sword.

"Your time is up!" she said. She calmly sliced off the Demon's
true head.

The Buffalo Demon had been killed – by a woman!

The gods cheered, and every living thing cheered too. The Buffalo Demon had been destroyed. Order was restored. Rivers flowed, fires burned, stars took their places in the sky, and the gods returned to Heaven.

Durga's ten arms became still. She closed her three eyes and smiled peacefully. One by one, gods and humans stepped forward and honoured her with flowers, perfume and gold.

"Supremely radiant Durga," they sang,
"protect us for ever.
Durga Demon-Slayer,
fill the universe with
your peace and power."

Prayers to Durga are still being sung in India today. And it is said that whoever recites them will never be alone.

Help me face this challenge,
slay the demons of fear.
Help me listen to my dreams,
show me self-confidence.
Give me the bravery of a beginner
and the courage to try new things.
Give me the desire to reach my goals
and the wisdom to go at my own pace.
Let me shine with my own light,
radiant and joyful in my power
as I face this challenge.

Based on a 6th-century
Sanskrit hymn to the
Hindu Goddess
Durga

The Maiden Knight and the Northern Lights

One morning Mergen called to his sister, "I'm going hunting."

Agu-Nogon watched her brother strap a bow and quiver of arrows to his back.

"Take care," she said. "It's so cold, the animals are hungry. They'll eat anything – including you!"

"Don't worry, little sis!" laughed Mergen. "I'm a great hunter, I'll catch something delicious for our supper pot." And he leapt on to his chestnut horse and galloped away across the snow.

Agu-Nogon collected an armful of wood, went into their hut and stoked up the fire. Then she set to work decorating a tall blue hat for Mergen to wear to the winter feast. She stitched the hat with strips of gold lace like rays of shining sun. She worked all day, waiting for Mergen to come home. But by nightfall he had not returned.

The moon rose and Agu-Nogon heard a whinnying sound. The chestnut
horse had returned – alone.

"Where's Mergen?" she asked.

The horse circled her.

"Has something happened to him?"

The horse pounded the ground with his hoof.

"I told him to be careful!" she cried. Then she rushed into the hut,
pulled on warm clothes, took a burning stick from the fire and leapt on to
the horse's back.

The horse carried Agu-Nogon across the snow, under the moon and through the forest. Agu-Nogon held the burning torch high, waving it to frighten away the wolves. They rode all night, and as dawn broke they came to some scraps of cloth and a pile of bones. Mergen had been devoured by a starving Siberian tiger.

Agu-Nogon fell to the ground weeping. She wept as she gathered her brother's bones and carried them home. She wept as she washed the bones in icy spring water. And she wept as she whispered prayers and wrapped the bones in a silken pouch.

Then she buried her face in the horse's mane.

"I wish we could bring Mergen back," she sobbed.

The horse tossed his head.

"Do you think there's a way?"

The horse snorted.

"I've heard that the Northern Lights can bring back the dead," said Agu-Nogon. "But they don't like using their magic."

The horse whinnied.

Ago-Nogon wiped the tears from her face.

"Maybe we can trick the Northern Lights into bringing Mergen back to life."

The horse neighed.

Agu-Nogon ran to the hut. She rummaged in the clothes-chest, found her brother's best clothes and put them on. She tied up her long hair and tucked it inside her brother's blue hat, then hung his dagger from her belt. She looked exactly like Mergen and was filled with his courage. She hid the silken pouch of bones under the horse's saddle, then flung herself on to the horse's back.

"To the Northern Lights!" she cried.

They rode north, and it grew colder. The forest was covered in icicles.

They passed a reindeer with his antlers tangled in a tree. Agu-Nogon climbed down from the horse, snapped off some branches and freed the reindeer's antlers.

"Run free," she said. And the reindeer darted away.

They left the shelter of the forest and galloped across endless snow.

They passed a goose pushing an egg with her beak, pushing the egg back into its warm nest. Agu-Nogon gently picked up the egg and placed it in the nest.

"Have lots of little ones," she said. And the goose settled down to brood her eggs.

They rode along an icy river and passed a huge fish, a sturgeon, flapping on the freezing river bank. Agu-Nogon flipped the fish back into the water.

"Swim out to sea," she said. And the sturgeon swam away.

They travelled north and came to an icy rainbow arching into the sky – the bridge to the Northern Lights. The air glittered, and ribbons of light crackled and danced around them. Agu-Nogon felt scared,

"I have no idea how to trick the Northern Lights," she said.

But the chestnut horse trotted up the rainbow into the sky, to a palace of swirling mist.

"GUESTS!" boomed a voice. "Welcome them, my daughters."

Twelve brilliant lights appeared. They circled Agu-Nogon and the horse and pulled them into the palace.

Girlish voices giggled, "What handsome guests!"

The twelve lights flickered, and there stood twelve shining girls, each lit with a different coloured light.

The voice boomed, "Feed the guests, my daughters."

A turquoise girl stepped forward, clapped her hands, and a shining bowl and silver ladle appeared. The Turquoise Girl tipped and poured the ladle in the air, and instantly the bowl filled with steaming stew.

The girl clapped her hands again and a bale of hay appeared for the horse.

Agu-Nogon ate the stew and the twelve girls whispered, "He would make a handsome husband!"

Agu-Nogon heard them, and suddenly had an idea.

The voice boomed, "I am the King of the Northern Lights!"

There was a flash of lightning and a man appeared, sparkling with a thousand points of light. His shining beard flowed to the floor, his radiant crown touched the ceiling.

"Why have you come?" he bellowed.

Agu-Nogon shielded her eyes, stepped forward and bowed.

"My name is Mergen," she said. "I am a great hunter, and I've come to marry one of your daughters."

"Who doesn't want to marry one of my girls!" laughed the king. Then he boomed, "BOOTS!"

A pair of boots appeared, boots made of solid iron.

"Wear these boots out in one night," cried the king, "and I might think about a wedding."

Agu-Nogon, the horse, and the boots were taken through the palace to a shimmering chamber. As soon as they were alone Agu-Nogon sighed,

"These boots are so heavy, I couldn't wear them out in one night. I couldn't wear them out in a hundred nights."

The horse tossed his head, as if he was trapped.

"You look like that poor trapped reindeer," said Agu-Nogon.

The horse carried on tossing his head.

"Do you think the reindeer could help us?" asked Agu-Nogon.

The horse became still.

So Agu-Nogon called, "Reindeer, reindeer, help me now!"

Before the echo of her voice had faded, there stood the reindeer. He stepped into the iron boots and dashed away, leaving behind a trail of sparks.

The reindeer galloped and galloped, wearing the iron boots all night long.

The next morning, Agu-Nogon bowed before the king and presented him with the boots – tattered and torn to shreds!

"Now, may I marry one of your daughters?" she asked.

The daughters glimmered hopefully. But the King of the Northern Lights boomed, "SACKS!"

Two bulky sacks appeared.

"Separate the seeds from the ashes in one night," said the king, "and I will think about a wedding."

Agu-Nogon peeped inside the sacks. Ashes and seeds were mixed together in a dirty mess.

"I couldn't separate the seeds from the ashes in one night," she cried, "or even a thousand nights!"

The horse pressed his nose against a sack, and tried to push it.

"You look like the goose trying to push her egg… Of course!" cried Agu-Nogon. "The goose!"

Agu-Nogon called, "Goose, goose, help me now."

There was a clucking and a honking and the goose appeared, with seven little goslings waddling after her! The goose and goslings began pecking at the seeds and ashes. Pecking, pecking and pecking, all night long.

The next morning Agu-Nogon bowed before the king and presented him with the sacks – ashes in one and seeds in the other!

"Now may I marry one of your daughters?"

The Turquoise Girl gleamed. But the king bellowed, "RING! I dropped my gold ring in the Milky Way. Find my ring by morning, and I will agree to the wedding."

Agu-Nogon stood on the rainbow bridge and looked down into the Milky Way. It was a never-ending river of stars, and Agu-Nogon began to cry.

"I couldn't get to the bottom of this river in one night or a million nights. I will never get my brother back."

The chestnut horse swished his tail against Agu-Nogon.

"Stop it," she said. But the horse flipped his tail harder and harder.

"Careful! You'll flip me into the river, just as I flipped the… sturgeon!"

Agu-Nogon called, "Sturgeon, sturgeon, help me now."

There was a splash and the sturgeon popped his head out of the starry river. Then the fish dived down into the sparkling Milky Way, down, down, through countless twinkling stars, all night long.

The next morning, Agu-Nogon bowed before the king and presented him with the ring – old, gold and still shiny!

"Well done, Mergen!" boomed the king. "You are indeed a great hunter. You may keep the ring, and you may marry one of my daughters."

Agu-Nogon bowed and held out the ring to the Turquoise Girl. The girl beamed and put the ring on her finger. The Turquoise Girl was so happy, but Agu-Nogon was absolutely terrified.

Agu-Nogon and the horse went to their chamber to prepare for the wedding.

"I hope my trick works," said Agu-Nogon, as she pulled the silken pouch of bones from under the horse's saddle and laid the white bones out on the floor. "I hope the Turquoise Girl will bring Mergen back to life." Agu-Nogon placed arm and leg bones, shoulder and hip bones, finger and toe bones, skull and spine out on the floor in the right order.

Then she climbed on to the chestnut horse, and rode away as fast as she could.

The Northern Lights waited and waited, but the bridegroom did not appear. The Turquoise Girl went to his chamber and knocked on the door. There was no reply. So she pushed open the door, and there, on the ground, she saw bones! White bones.

"Mergen!" cried the Turquoise Girl. "Oh my Mergen! What has happened to you!"

The Turquoise girl clapped her hands and the silver ladle appeared. She held the silver ladle over the bones and began to tip and pour. Silver liquid poured on to the bones and they began to move. The bones drew themselves together and began to mend. The ladle tipped. Flesh covered bones and skin covered flesh. The ladle poured.

Breath flowed, fingers twitched, and eyes opened. Mergen sat up, whole and healed and alive! The Turquoise Girl hugged him with relief.

Mergen rubbed his eyes,

"Where am I?" he said.

"With the Northern Lights, of course!" laughed the Turquoise girl. "Remember? It's your wedding day!"

"Wedding!" said Mergen. "All I remember is a hungry Siberian tiger."

"Don't you remember the iron boots? The sacks? The ring?"

Mergen shook his head. He looked around. The shimmering chamber was empty except for a tall blue hat decorated with strips of gold lace.

"How did my hat get here?" he asked.

"You arrived wearing it."

Mergen stood up,

"Something is wrong," he said.

The Turquoise Girl looked at Mergen. He was much taller and even more handsome than before.

"Yes," she replied, "something is very wrong – there are two Mergens!"

"I think I know who the other one is," said Mergen. "Come on, we must find her!"

The Turquoise Girl grabbed Mergen by the hand and whirled him
into the air. They flew through the palace and over the snow looking
for Agu-Nogon. In the distance they saw the chestnut horse with
Agu-Nogon, galloping away.

"Stop, little sis!" shouted Mergen. "It's me – your brother –
I'm alive!"

Agu-Nogon pulled up the horse.

"Brother?" she cried in amazement. "Have you really come back?"
She threw her arms around his neck. Then she looked shyly at the
Turquoise Girl.

"I am sorry I tricked you," she said, untying her long hair, "I'm not
Mergen – I'm his sister."

The Turquoise Girl looked from brother to sister and back again,
and began to laugh.

"I don't know what we are going to tell Father," she said.

Mergen took both girls' hands.

"Don't worry," he said. "I will explain everything."

Mergen bowed before the King of the Northern Lights.

"I am the real Mergen," he said, "and this is my sister. She is a maiden,
but her heart is as brave as a knight's. Because of her courage I've been

brought back to life. We ask for your forgiveness."

"Forgiveness!" boomed the king. "What about the wedding?"

Mergen bowed to the Turquoise Girl.

"I don't know anything about boots, sacks and rings, but will you marry me?"

The Turquoise Girl shone with happiness, then turned to Agu-Nogon and said, "Thank you, maiden knight. Your courage has brought me a husband – and a sister!"

The Turquoise Girl clapped her hands and the magic ladle appeared. She placed the ladle in Agu-Nogon's hands.

"This is yours now. Tip, and pour your own future."

Then there was a wedding.

And the Northern Lights flashed and danced so brightly, they were seen all over the world.

Amazon Accessories

Make a bag and decorate it with cut-out shapes.

Brighten up an old T-shirt with coloured dye.

Decorate a paper fan.

Customise a belt using a glue-gun, glitter and sequins.

Thread beads to make jewellery.

Get someone to show you how to knit.

Using coloured silk, embroider a pattern on your scarf.

Hand of Glory

Effie got all the worst jobs. She was the first up to light the fires, and last to sleep when she had finished the washing-up. And she didn't even have a bed. She had to curl up in a blanket beside the fire. Life as a servant girl was hard work. But the innkeeper was a kind man, and The Traveller's Repose was a kind of home.

The Traveller's Repose was the only inn on the Yorkshire Moors, and if you had been riding all day it was a welcome sight. Travellers could eat, drink and sleep, and there was plenty of hay for their horses.

Effie liked it best once she had served dinner and the guests relaxed around the fire. They would often tell tales of their travels: getting lost on the moors in thick Yorkshire mist, seeing the ghost of the Headless Rider, or narrowly escaping a band of brutal highwaymen.

One night, as Effie was curling up in her blanket, she was startled by a loud banging at the door. She rushed to pull back the iron bolts, and there, huddled from the wind and rain, was an old lady.

"Child," begged the old woman, "let me in. It's cruel out here."

The old lady was all wrapped up in a bonnet and shawl, and was carrying a big black bag. "Let me in, do. I've been walking over the moor all night. I thought I'd never find shelter."

"The beds are all taken," said Effie. "But you're welcome to warm yourself by the fire."

"That would be grand," said the old lady.

Effie pulled a chair up to the fire, brought a plate of bread and cheese, and poured a glass of milk from the jug. The old woman ate and drank, then settled back and closed her eyes.

Effie yawned. She was too tired to wash the plate and put the jug of milk back in the larder. She lay down by the fire, next to the old woman's feet. She was just curling up in her blanket, when she noticed something strange: the old woman had big feet, very big feet, and she was wearing a pair of men's boots! Effie felt something was not right. So she half-closed her eyes, pretended to snore, and peeped out through her eye-lashes.

She watched the old lady stand up, take off her old lady's wig and remove her old lady's dress. Underneath was an evil-looking man with dirty clothes and scars across his cheeks! Effie nearly gasped with fright, but managed to disguise it as a yawn.

The evil-looking man reached into the big, black bag and rummaged around. There was a squelching sound, and he pulled something white and waxy out of the bag. It was a hand – a human hand – the hand of a dead man!

Effie nearly choked with terror, but managed to disguise it as a snore.

Effie watched as the evil-looking man put the dead hand upright on the table, then took a tinderbox from his bag and struck a light. He touched the light to each finger and to the thumb, lighting them as if they were candles. The fingers and thumb shone. The dead hand burned brightly.

Then the man muttered in a low voice.

"Hand of Glory, Hand of Glory, Let those who sleep Be asleep. Let those who wake Be awake."

The hand gleamed, and a thin wisp of smoke curled from the tips of the fingers and swirled across the room. The smoke floated up the wooden staircase to the bedrooms. It slipped under the bedroom doors and into the nostrils of the innkeeper and the sleeping guests. Everyone who had been asleep was now deeply asleep. So deeply asleep, it was as if they were dead. But Effie had been awake and was now more awake than she had ever been. She could see and hear everything.

The evil-looking man went to the door, pulled back the bolts and whistled loudly. In came four more men, each with a sack on his back.

"Boss!" they cried. "That Hand of Glory works a treat. Now to business."

Effie watched the men fill their sacks with silver knives and forks from the kitchen and fine linen from the dining-room.

"Over here, lads," shouted one robber, pointing to the clock on the mantelpiece and the pistols crossed above the fireplace.

"Give us a hand, boys!" cried another, as he pulled a picture from the wall.

The robbers didn't even try to be quiet. They were sure that the Hand of Glory had put everyone to sleep.

All the time the hand burned, and all the time Effie lay awake watching. She knew that she had to put the Hand of Glory out.

When the robbers had stolen everything downstairs, they went upstairs to the bedrooms, and Effie crept quietly into the kitchen. She filled a bucket with water and tipped it over the burning hand. As the water touched the hand, the flames shot up like long red fingernails. Water did not put out the fire: the hand burned more brightly!

Upstairs, the robbers went from room to room. They emptied wallets, stole watches from night-stands, ripped jewellery from ladies' necks, stole travelling bags and purses. The Hand of Glory was so powerful that the robbers even dug a gold filling out of the innkeeper's back tooth. He was so deeply asleep, he heard and felt nothing.

"How can I put the fire out...?" thought Effie. "I'll smother it!"

Effie threw her apron over the Hand of Glory. As the apron covered the hand, the flames leapt higher, like jagged tongues of fire. Smothering did not put out the fire: the hand burned more fiercely!

"The only way to put out these flames," thought Effie, "is to undo the spell. Maybe if I whisper the spell backwards, it will work."

So Effie muttered:

"Awake be,
wake who those let,
Asleep be,
sleep who those let.
Glory of hand,
Glory of hand."

But the flames blazed so violently, they nearly reached the ceiling.

"Oh! oh, oh!" wept Effie. "How can I put out the Hand of Glory?"

Just at that moment, the robbers started coming down the stairs.

"That's the lot, boys," called the robber chief. "We've got all the booty now."

Effie looked about in desperation and saw the jug of milk still on the table.

Not knowing what else to do, she picked up the jug and dashed milk over the flaming hand.

As the white milk splashed the burning hand, the flames shrank, the flames became smaller and smaller and the waxy hand melted away. The white bones crumbled and the flames went out. The Hand of Glory was nothing but a pile of ashes in a pool of milk.

Instantly, everyone woke up. Effie heard shouting and banging as the innkeeper and guests struggled with the robbers, forcing them to the ground and binding their hands tight.

The guests pulled on their dressing-gowns and gathered downstairs, and the innkeeper emptied the sacks of stolen goods on to the floor.

"How did this happen?" he said. "I wake up at the slightest noise, yet tonight I was deeply asleep. It was almost as if the Hand of Glory was upon me."

Effie spoke in a small voice,

"The Hand of Glory *was* upon you, sir." And she pointed to the table.

The guests stared at the ashes and the milk, and the innkeeper shook his head in disbelief.

"How did you put out the Hand of Glory?" he asked.

"I tried everything, sir," said Effie. "Nothing worked, until I poured milk over the Hand."

"You're a brave lass, Effie. And you did the right thing. The Hand of Glory is the hand of a hanged man – a criminal. It's a dark spell, truly bad. There's only one thing that'll put out its fire, and that's milk, pure innocent milk, mother's food – something truly good."

"Three cheers for Effie," shouted the guests, "who broke the spell and saved us all!"

They lifted Effie on to their shoulders and danced her round the room.

Effie grinned. She had never felt so truly good!

The innkeeper promoted Effie from serving girl to cook, and gave her a proper bedroom and money in her pocket each week. Effie still liked it best when she had finished cooking and the guests relaxed around the fire and told tales. But the tale they wanted to hear now was the story of the Hand of Glory.

As for the robbers – they were hanged. And as they swung dead from the gallows, other robbers crept up in the darkness, took out their knives, and cut off the hanged men's hands…

"Hand of Glory,
Hand of Glory,
Let those who sleep
Be asleep.
Let those who wake
Be awake."

Be an Amazon

Practise

Have fun

Dare to dream

The Warrior Princess

What Princess Al-Datma liked to do best was gallop fast on her black horse, fight with a sword, and beat her father at chess.

Al-Datma's mother had died when she was a baby, and her father brought her up. He adored the little princess and taught her how to ride, how to hold a bow and arrow, how to hunt and fight.

By the time Al-Datma was eighteen years old she was a skilled warrior and a great beauty. Her face was round like the moon, she had dark eyebrows that arched over glittering eyes, and her mouth was red as a pomegranate. There was no other girl in the kingdom as bold and beautiful as the Warrior Princess.

One day, Al-Datma said to her father, "It's time for me to get married."

The king smiled. "I quite agree."

"But I will only marry my equal," said the princess.

"Absolutely, my daughter. There are plenty of rich and handsome princes –"

"No, Father," interrupted Al-Datma. "I will only marry the man who can beat me at riding, sword-fighting and playing chess. The man who succeeds, I will happily marry. But the man who fails, will be branded on his forehead with the words: *I fought Al-Datma and lost*."

"Dear girl!" exclaimed the king. "That's rather nasty, isn't it?"

"Nasty, Father? No, it's kind. The whole kingdom will know such men are fools, and can avoid them."

Soon there was a long queue of men waiting at the palace gates, hoping to marry Al-Datma. They stood in line grooming horses, polishing shields, practising sword-skills and playing chess.

When the gates opened, the young man at the head of the queue climbed on to his horse and rode into the palace to meet the Warrior Princess.

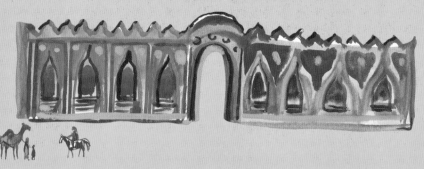

Al-Datma was already mounted on her black horse, dressed in full armour.

"If that's a horse," she cried, "then catch me!" And she galloped off.

The young man chased after her, but his horse was left far behind.

"That's not a horse," shouted Al-Datma, "it's a snail! Bring me the branding iron."

A red-hot branding iron was brought. The princess pressed the iron on to the young man's forehead. There was a sizzling sound and the smell of singeing flesh, and there, burnt black on the young man's brow, were the words, 'I fought Al-Datma and lost'.

"Now everyone will know what a good rider you are!" she laughed.

One by one the young men went to meet Al-Datma, but none of them passed the first test. The princess rode faster than all of them and branded them with her fire, until the kingdom was filled with the words, 'I fought Al-Datma and lost'.

The queue of men waiting at the gates vanished. No one wanted to marry the princess – she was too scary. News of the Warrior Princess travelled all the way to Persia. King Behram, like all Persian kings before him, was a skilled horseman, a great warrior, and excelled at playing chess. But he was lonely. And when he heard about Al-Datma, he gathered his advisors and announced: "We're going to Egypt. Princess Al-Datma is just the girl for me."

"Hardly, Your Majesty!" mumbled the advisors. "She has branded every single one of her suitors."

"That's what I mean," laughed Behram, "she's got spirit. Make preparations for the journey at once."

Al-Datma's father gave a warm welcome to his honoured Persian guest. He thought King Behram was kind and handsome, and couldn't help feeling it was a shame that Behram's good looks would be spoiled by the branding iron. But King Behram was determined to beat Al-Datma, and rode out to meet her. The Princess was dressed in armour from head to toe and called out to him: "I am the Warrior Princess! Turn back before I brand you." And she galloped off on her black horse.

Behram raced after her, urging his horse to go faster and faster. Al-Datma looked over her shoulder – the gap was closing between them – Behram had nearly caught up with her. She leant into her horse's neck, driving it on. Behram stood up in his saddle – his horse gave an enormous leap – and landed ahead!

Behram had passed the first test: he had beaten the Warrior Princess at riding.

Behram drew his sword.

"Call that a sword?" cried Al-Datma. "It's a blunt pin!" And she flashed her own sharp sword through the air.

Their swords clashed. Al-Datma fought with strong, precise strikes. Behram parried and dodged, blocking her blows. Al-Datma used all her power, thrusting and jabbing. But Behram fought back, swinging and clashing. Then Behram slipped his sword underneath Al-Datma's sword and with a grin, placed his sword gently across her neck!

King Behram had passed the second test: he had beaten the Warrior Princess at sword-fighting.

They walked back to the palace in silence. Al-Datma peered at Behram through her visor. He was a talented rider, a skilled swordsman, and she had to admit that he was very handsome. She wondered if he was any good at chess.

When they sat down at the chess board, Al-Datma was not wearing her suit of armour. She wore a scarlet dress, her black hair loose over her shoulders, her face covered with a fine gold veil.

"You think your mind is big enough to beat me at chess?" she taunted. "A closed room cannot compete with the open sky!"

Al-Datma swooped on the board and began to capture Behram's pieces one by one. But Behram's play was strategic and his moves clever. They played long into the night, and Behram began to win. He captured Al-Datma's queen, and moved towards her king. Al-Datma was not pleased – she was the Warrior Princess and could not be beaten. She slowly lifted her golden veil, flashed her eyes and smiled at King Behram.

Behram gazed in wonder. Her face was round like the moon, dark eyebrows arched over glittering eyes, and her mouth was red as a pomegranate. He stared at her face and felt he could look for ever. Behram was so bewildered by her beauty that, as he stretched his hand towards the chess board, he could not stop looking at the princess's face, and made the wrong move.

Al-Datma laughed, pounced on the chessboard and took his king.

"Checkmate!" she cried. "I've won. The Warrior Princess has beaten you at chess!"

Behram smiled. "You are fair to look upon, lady," he said. "But you do not play fair."

"Of course I play fair," said the princess grandly. "And to prove it, as you won two of the tests, I won't brand you."

Behram bowed and took his leave.

King Behram's advisors rushed to his side,

"Your Majesty, we must return home at once," they said, "before this woman destroys you."

"Go home?" replied Behram. "Never! She has already destroyed me. I am in love."

Behram went to see Al-Datma's father.

"I am not pleased with my daughter," said the king, shaking his head. "She has turned away a charming suitor. The warrior arts have led her down a lonely path. I hardly dare speak to her myself these days, in case she brands me!"

Al-Datma sat in her chamber and thought about Behram – she liked him, she missed him, but she'd sent him away.

The princess's serving maids tried to cheer her.

"Sword practice, Your Highness?"

Al-Datma put on her armour and went out to compete, but she felt empty inside.

One morning Al-Datma looked out of her window and saw a ragged, bearded merchant spreading a cloth on the grass and laying out his wares, covering the cloth with twinkling jewels.

"Let's see what he's selling!" cried the serving maids.

Al-Datma followed her serving maids into the garden.

"What beautiful things!" said the maids, falling on the jewels. They examined ruby brooches, glittering hair pins, tinkling anklets, ivory combs and a tiara studded with diamonds. They combed out Al-Datma's hair, fixed it with pins, hung pearls from her ears and gold at her throat, and placed the tiara on her head.

The merchant pulled a mirror from his sack and rubbed it on his dirty rags. "You look like the sun, moon and stars," he said, lifting the mirror to her face.

Al-Datma turned this way and that, admiring the jewels.

"How much do they cost?" she asked.

"These jewels are expensive," said the merchant. "They come all the way from Persia."

"Persia!" exclaimed Al-Datma. "I will take the lot."

"They are not to be bought for money," said the merchant.

"So what do you want for them?" asked the princess.

"One hundred kisses, my lady."

The princess was horrified. A hundred kisses! Kissing that grubby beggar once would be too much.

"My maid servants will kiss you," she declared.

"Then there is no sale," said the merchant.

Al-Datma gazed at the jewels. She had to have them.

"Gather round," she whispered to her maid servants. "Spread out your skirts and shield me, so no one can see."

Al-Datma held her nose, stood on tip-toe, and kissed the merchant on his greasy, hairy cheek.

"One!" giggled the maid servants, and they began to count. "Two... three... ten..." The counting got louder – "fifteen... twenty... twenty-five..." – and louder.

The sound rose from the garden, to the king's ears.

"... thirty-three... forty..."

"What is going on?" cried the king. And he hurried into the garden. He saw the serving maids, standing in a circle chanting, "... fifty-five... sixty..."

"Do be quiet!" he shouted. "I'm trying to work."

But the maids continued, "... seventy-nine... eighty..."

"Out of my way!" cried the king.

But the girls kept counting.

"... ninety-one... ninety-three..."

The king pushed through the circle

"... ninety-five..."

and saw his daughter kissing a strange-looking man with a very crumpled beard.

"... ninety-nine..."

"STOP!" cried the king. "I've had enough. You rejected the King of Persia, and yet you kiss this ragged merchant. You obviously consider this man to be your equal – you can marry him. And since you have chosen a merchant, you can leave my palace at once."

The merchant packed up the jewels, took Al-Datma's hand and led her through the palace gates and out into the dusty streets. Al-Datma began to cry.

"What's the matter now?" said the merchant roughly.

"I wish I'd married King Behram," stammered the princess.

"But he failed the tests," said the merchant.

Al-Datma sniffed,

"He beat me at riding, he beat me at sword-fighting, and he would have beaten me at chess..."

"Except?" said the merchant.

"Except," sobbed the princess, "I could not bear to lose. So I tricked him."

"How?" asked the merchant fiercely.

"I showed him my face," cried Al-Datma. "But now I realise that winning was losing, and I have lost the most precious thing of all – the one I love." Tears ran down Al-Datma's cheeks.

"Have you a handkerchief?" asked the merchant.

The princess fumbled in her pocket and pulled out a delicate linen handkerchief. She was about to blow her nose, when the merchant grabbed the handkerchief.

"Let me show you my face," he said, wiping the clean handkerchief over his greasy face. Then he tugged at his beard and ripped it off.

Underneath was King Behram!

Al-Datma gazed at him in wonder, and felt that she could look for ever. Finally she said, "You are fair to look upon, my lord, but you do not play fair."

King Behram knelt in the dust and took her hand,

"Forgive me, but you are the Warrior Princess, and as you won by trickery, I could only win you by tricking you back."

At last, Al-Datma had met her equal.

Now it's your turn — go out and be an Amazon!

About the Stories

For more about Amazons, look at:

On the Trail of the Women Warriors, Lyn Webster Wilde (Constable & Co, 1999).

Warrior Women: An Archaeologist's Search for History's Hidden Heroines, Jeannine Davis-Kimball and Mona Behan (Time Warner International, 2002).

The Encyclopedia of Amazons: Women Warriors from Antiquity to the Modern Era, Jessica Amanda Salmonson (Paragon House Publishers, 1991).

Woman Warrior, Fact or Tale, Sally Pomme Clayton (Estudos Literatura Oral, Journal 7-8, 2002).

Queen of the Amazons

There are many versions of this story. I have made my own pathway through the myth, taking liberties with the ending. Some of the versions can be found in *Greek Myths*, Robert Graves (Penguin Books).

Dragon Girl

There is a Chinese song called *The Ballad of Li Chi*. And look out for the amazing story of the goddess Tianhou.

Chinese Fairy Tales and Fantasies, translated and edited by Moss Roberts (Pantheon Books, 1979).

Winning Eagle Feathers

Counting coup is an ancient Native American tradition.

American Indian Myths and Legends, Richard Erdoes and Alfonso Ortiz (Pantheon Books, 1984).

Durga Demon-Slayer

Durga is a beloved goddess in India and many shrines are dedicated to her. The spell is based on ancient hymns still being sung today.

Indian Mythology: An Encyclopaedia of Myth and Legend, Jan Knappert (The Aquarian Press, 1991).

The Maiden Knight and the Northern Lights

Tales about a girl who saves her brother often appear in Siberian literature. There are many variations on the magic journey she makes.

The Oral Epic of Siberia and Central Asia, G.M.H. Schoolbraid (Indiana University Press, 1975).

Mergen and His Friends: a Nanai folk tale, translated by James Riordan (Progress Publishers, 1973).

Hand of Glory

The idea of using a dead man's hand to put people to sleep is found throughout Europe. I have been telling the story for many years and this version comes from Yorkshire, where you can see a real Hand of Glory in Whitby Museum!

There are great versions of the story in:

Clever Gretchen and Other Forgotten Folktales, Alison Lurie (HarperCollins, 1980).

English Folk and Other Fairy Tales, Edwin Sidney Hartland (Walter Scott Publishing Company, 1890).

The Warrior Princess

Middle Eastern literature abounds with warrior women. An Arabic story was the source for this tale:

Arabian Nights, a selection (Penguin Popular Classics, 1997).

The story is similar to European tales such as Grimm's *King Thrushbeard*, Hans Christian Anderson's *The Swineherd*, and Shakespeare's *The Taming of the Shrew*.

Thanks from Sally Pomme Clayton to Lyn Webster Wilde, who continues to show what it means to be an Amazon.

Thanks from Sophie Herxheimer to Panni Bharti for insight into Durga and Sanskrit script, Charlotte Herxheimer for the Chinese characters, Dima Jarkas for the Arabic script, and Fotios Begklis for the Greek script.

Glossary

米 (Chinese) – rice

酒 (Chinese) – wine

天保 (Chinese) – Heaven protect, Earth protect

दुर्गा- स्तुति (Hindi) – a hymn to Durga

قاتلت الدغماء وحسرت (Arabic) – I fought Al-Datma and lost